Chuong Van Nguyen

The Seed of God

Chuong Van Nguyen

Copyright Page

The Seed of God
Author: Chuong Van Nguyen

Copyright © 2024 by Authors Sphere Inc.
All rights reserved.

No part of this publication may be reproduced, distributed, or transmitted in any form or by any means, including photocopying, recording, or other electronic or mechanical methods, without the prior written permission of the publisher, except in the case of brief quotations embodied in critical reviews and certain other noncommercial uses permitted by copyright law. For permission requests, please contact the publisher at the address below.

Published by Authors Sphere Inc.
99 Wall Street, New York, NY 10005, USA

This is a work of fiction. Names, characters, places, and incidents either are products of the author's imagination or are used fictitiously. Any resemblance to actual events, locales, or persons, living or dead, is entirely coincidental.

Chuong Van Nguyen

Once, there was a time when a young research scientist named Doug studied and created ways to enhance plant life. He was a plant biologist, relatively new to the workforce environment, having worked in the field for several months.

While Doug worked in the lab, he often found himself bored, contemplating ways to innovate and create new forms of plant life. One day, he conceived an intriguing idea: merging cells from different plants to create a completely new organism. Excited by this notion, he began planning and gathering various plants for his experiment.

After some research and purchases from florists and fruit shops, and online orders, Doug collected the necessary plant parts at his home lab. As he awaited the arrival of the remaining plants, weeks passed, and finally, all packages arrived.

Doug proceeded with merging the plant cells into a single entity.

He carefully planted the merged cells, which he referred to as his "seed," in a pot filled with soil in his backyard. Hoping for success, Doug eagerly awaited results, knowing that no one had attempted such an experiment before.

Unfortunately, after a couple of months, Doug saw no signs of growth in his experiment. Disheartened, he felt like a failure and considered abandoning his dream of creating new life. He believed his invention to be impossible and regretted investing so much time and effort into it.

Feeling dejected, Doug retired to his couch, berating himself for pursuing what now seemed like a futile endeavor. Eventually, he went to bed, oblivious to the heavy rains and thunderstorms that ensued.

During the storm, lightning struck directly at Doug's potted plant. Miraculously, the plant began to grow rapidly, absorbing the rainwater and breaking the pot with its overgrown roots. The growth stopped suddenly, leaving Doug's backyard transformed overnight.

The next morning, tired and groggy, Doug noticed the unusual growth from his window and rushed outside in disbelief. "Wow, it worked after all!" he exclaimed, marveling at the unexpected outcome.

Examining the plant closely, Doug pondered what had triggered its sudden growth. He recalled the thunderstorm and realized that the lightning strike might have given life to his experiment. Observing the plant's unusual purplish-green color, Doug felt a mix of nervousness and excitement about its future development.

Repairing the damaged pot and planting the growing tree in his backyard, Doug continued to monitor its progress. Although initially unsure if the plant would continue to grow, Doug left for a while to run errands, hoping for further growth upon his return. To his surprise, the plant had grown significantly larger and bore fruits in his absence. It seemed to

thrive more when he was away.

That very day, Doug had come back home, put all his grocery bags on the table, and went into his backyard to check up on his plant. He couldn't believe how quickly it had grown. The tree had an unusual-colored fruit on it. He saw two different colored fruits, which was quite odd. One fruit was blue, and the other was red. The fruits seemed unusual but tempting to eat. He needed to examine them first to see if they were poisonous. So, he plucked the two-colored fruits from the tree and brought them inside for further tests. After examining them, he found no indication of toxicity.

He attempted to try them but didn't know which one to start with. After some thought, he decided to taste the blue one. He took a bite, chewed, and then swallowed it. At first, it tasted weird and funny, but the more he chewed, the better it tasted. Suddenly, he started to feel high and collapsed to the ground. He fainted.

Moments later, he awoke and got back up. He was confused, not remembering what had happened until he turned around and saw himself still lying on the floor.

"Is that me? What's going on here? Am I dead? Did the fruit I just ate kill me?"

He remembered examining the fruit and found no indication of poison. Then a sudden miracle started happening. He slowly began to float in the air, going upwards straight through his house and heading to the skies. He felt scared, not knowing what was going on or where he was going.

He kept floating upwards until he reached the clouds. Suddenly, he stopped there. He wasn't going anywhere else but was standing there, feeling weird and confused. He was all by himself, seeing no one around him in the distance. He started to walk slowly, taking baby steps, afraid he might fall from the bubbling clouds. The more he walked, the more he got the hang of it. He kept walking until he saw a giant gate. He went towards it, and the gate automatically opened for him.

He stood there for a moment, feeling nervously confused, not knowing what or where the entrance would lead. He assumed this must be heaven and that he had died from eating that fruit.

"I must be truly dead; this is why I'm here!" he said.

He continued to walk until suddenly, out of nowhere, a voice could be heard speaking to him.

"Who's there?" Doug asked.

"I'm an Angel, and I'm here to guide you!" the voice replied. The Angel then appeared closer to him.

"You are in heaven," said the Angel.

"Damn, that means I'm dead!" Doug exclaimed.

"No, you're not," the Angel said.

"So, why am I here then?" Doug asked.

"You're not dead but temporarily blacked out," explained the Angel. "You've only got a limited time here, and you'll be returning back to Earth where your body is. Come with me, and I will show you around the kingdom of heaven and introduce you to God himself."

"Wow, would I be meeting God?" Doug asked enthusiastically.

He was very enthusiastic about meeting God and couldn't wait. He wondered what God would look like.

While walking along the path, Doug was very excited about heaven. He always wanted to be there.

"It is very beautiful," he said. "What a palace, with nice shining sunlight appearing across it with rainbow colors."

He could see people and other Angels everywhere as he walked past them. The Angel then escorted him into a chamber filled with delicious-looking food. Everything looked immaculate and well-catered. The Angel left him there to enjoy his feast and would come to get him back once he was full.

Doug couldn't wait any longer and dug in. He devoured all the fruit that looked good to eat, including some he had never seen before.

"It tastes very good," he remarked.

After that, he went to the meat section and devoured everything there. He became full and was very satisfied with the meal. The Angel that had escorted him earlier came back once he was done eating. He came to take him into another chamber. Doug wondered what it would be like this time, besides the food. As soon as he entered another chamber, he saw the Angel introducing many women to him.

"Wow, they all look so beautiful," Doug said.

"They're all yours, and you can do whatever you want with them," said the Angel.

The Angel once again left him alone with the women for a while. He enjoyed sleeping with them and had fun. As time passed, he suddenly felt exhausted and went to sleep on the bed with the girls he had just been with. Hours later, the Angel came to Doug and woke him up, asking him to come with him again. Doug was full of surprises and didn't know what would happen next until he was told it was time to meet God.

"Oh, yeah, right, I forgot about that. I was too busy with the girls and got tired all of a sudden," Doug said.

As they walked and reached the point where they were to meet God, everyone was waiting. Doug was very surprised to see who was standing right next to him. It was Jesus.

"Jesus, is that you?" he asked.

"Yes, it is. I am Jesus, the Son of God," Jesus replied.

"Wow, it's a pleasure to meet you," Doug said. "So, you're real after all, not a fictional character made up by man. And may I ask, did you really get tortured and crucified?"

"Yes," said Jesus, "what you have heard about me is true in the Bible, and it is also rude to ask me that question."

Doug continued to ask Jesus more questions about him, but Jesus interrupted and told him, "God is arriving. Here he is now!"

"Oh, okay, but where is he?" Doug asked.

"I see nothing but a bright light shining in my face."

Jesus and the others were able to see God's physical presence, but Doug could not.

God suddenly spoke. "How are you, my son?"

Doug didn't know who God was speaking to until the others told him it was him.

"Oh, me, I'm good, thank you!" Doug replied.

"How is heaven?" God asked. "Are you enjoying it so far?"

"Yes, yes I am. It's such a pleasure and a paradise here!" Doug said. "But may I ask, how come I'm unable to see your appearance?"

"My son, I cannot reveal my true image to you as you're not ready yet to see what I really look like," God explained. "I will not let you expose the truth of what I look like to the world. When the time comes, I will show you."

"But I'm already in heaven. Who am I going to spread the word around to? Everybody here can see you," Doug said.

"As the Angel explained earlier, you're not actually dead but temporarily blacked out and fainted. You're only staying here for a short period of time. You'll return to Earth after our conversation is over. There are more important things I need to explain to you before you go back," God said.

"Oh, I thought I'd died permanently," Doug said.

"No, you didn't. And listen, the fruit you ate, the blue one, is the key to heaven. The red one leads down to Hell. Never eat that one, or you'll be visiting Hell and might never return home again."

"Thanks for letting me know, God. Luckily, I chose and ate the right fruit; otherwise, I would have gone to Hell first instead of Heaven, and who knows what would have happened there," Doug said.

"See this staff here?" God asked. "This is no ordinary staff; it's called Heaven's Staff and could never be taken away by any means."

"What does the staff do?" Doug asked.

"The staff can eliminate any living thing on Earth with a swing. It can also kill any demons from Hell. It is a weapon that can destroy," God explained.

"This staff can open up Hell on Earth, so it must never be taken away or used."

"I understand," Doug said. "But why are you so keen to tell me all this about the staff? I'm not going to be here very long. What difference does it make when I return home?"

"The reason I'm telling you this is because you now have the blue fruit planted in your backyard," God told him. "You can come to heaven very often whenever you feel like it and roam the kingdom, but just don't touch the Heaven's Staff when you're visiting."

"Oh, I see now, understood!" Doug said. "Just asking, why do I feel like all this is a dream? Can you prove to me that this is not a dream and make me feel like this is real? Can you make my body slim? I hate being overweight. I have always been the fat one ever since I was a kid until now. Prove to me that I'm not dreaming and make me a skinny person. Can you help me do that?"

"Okay, I'll give you your wish. Take this special bean, and you will lose the fat in no time, but not here in heaven. Take the bean with you to Earth, as your actual body is there. If you eat the bean now, your soul cannot lose the weight, and it will make no difference," God said.

"Got it, God. Is there anything else I should know before I return?" Doug asked.

"Remember what I told you about eating the red fruit. It leads to Hell, and it is no paradise there. The three devils down there are very evil and experts at making lies to manipulate people into believing them," God warned.

"Three?" Doug said. "I thought there was only one with two horns

That day, while working next to his closest colleague named Quad, Doug couldn't keep his secrets to himself about what he had discovered over the past few months. So, he went ahead and told him everything in confidence.

He explained everything about the new plant he had discovered and how he went to heaven by eating the fruit from it. But Quad didn't believe his story.

"If you don't believe me, then how do you explain my weight loss in such a short period of time?" Doug asked.

He further explained about the bean given to him by God, which made him slim by eating it.

"If you don't believe me, then come with me to my house, and I'll show you what I have discovered!"

Later that day, at the end of their shift, Quad decided to go with Doug to see for himself. A few moments later, they arrived by car. Doug showed Quad to his backyard and the tree he was talking about.

"There, see what I've created!" Doug said. "Beautiful, isn't it?"

"To actually believe me, let's go to heaven now by eating the fruit," Doug continued. "Eating the fruit is the keyway to heaven."

"And what does the red fruit lead to?" Quad asked.

"Oh, you wouldn't want to eat that one; it leads to Hell!" Doug replied. "That's the bad one, and it can never be eaten by any means. Is that clear?"

Quad understood. They both went ahead and took a bite out of the blue fruit, with Quad first and then Doug. They both collapsed to the floor, their souls leaving their bodies and ascending to Heaven. Suddenly, they found themselves in the clouds.

"Come on, this way," Doug said. "I'll lead the way for you. I've been here before, so don't worry; I know exactly where I'm going."

Quad took baby steps, afraid he might fall.

"It's alright," said Doug. "Keep walking, and you'll be fine. I was the same way when I first got here."

Quad kept walking and finally got used to it. While walking the path to the kingdom, they reached the entrance. The gate automatically opened for them.

"Now do you believe everything I told you?" Doug asked.

"Sure, I believe you now!" Quad replied.

However, Quad wasn't truly amused. He pretended to be happy, hiding his true feelings. As they made their way in, Doug guided him around, but Quad didn't seem too impressed. Doug noticed something was wrong and became suspicious. Quad pretended to smile, but Doug wasn't convinced. He continued to show him around.

Later, they enjoyed their time with women and had a feast together. They spent a lot of time in the kingdom. After hours of joy, the two were being chased by beautiful girls. They ran across the staff section, which was forbidden to enter.

"What's that stick floating in that chamber?" Quad asked.

"Oh, that is the staff," Doug replied. "The staff is prohibited and cannot be taken or used for any purpose. It's priceless."

"Okay, understood," Quad said. "Can we go back home now?"

"What's the matter? Aren't you enjoying heaven?" Doug asked.

"Yeah, it's good and everything, but I'd rather be back on earth. Heaven's not really for me at this point in time," Quad said.

"Wow, if it were me, I'd want to stay here for the rest of eternity," Doug replied.

"Anyway, it's just a temporary stay here. The fruit allows only a small amount of time in heaven. We should be heading back soon."

Moments later, their time in heaven was up, and they returned to earth. They woke up back in their bodies. "Wow, it feels like a dream we just had," Quad said.

"Yeah, it does!" Doug replied.

Doug then had to go to the toilet and told Quad to wait for him in the lounge. When he was done, he went out to check on him but couldn't find him anywhere. He looked all over the house until he went to the backyard. He was shocked to see Quad lying on the ground with the red fruit in his hand.

"You idiot, what have you done? You took a bite out of it! Now you're really going to Hell!" Doug exclaimed.

He picked him up and brought him to the lounge to rest on the couch. He didn't know whether Quad would return later or be gone forever, so he waited to see what would happen.

While Quad was on his way to Hell, he initially saw darkness, then suddenly flames burst everywhere. Assuming he had reached Hell's boundaries, he nervously walked around, not knowing where to go.

He saw demon soldiers torturing and butchering people alive. Unsure of what to think, he kept walking and saw other people being tortured in many ways. A demon pointed the way, and Quad followed the path to where the devil sat on a throne.

"I was expecting you," said the Devil. "I was expecting someone like you to show up down here."

"So, you know who I am, and you've been waiting for me this whole time?" Quad replied. "Precisely."

"I always wanted to come here my entire life," Quad said. "I have worshiped you secretly."

"I know, and it's good to hear that from you. So, what's the reason you want to be here?" the Devil asked.

"It's to serve you, my master! And who are the other two sitting beside you?"

"There are three of us Devils!"

"What? Really? I never knew that! I thought there was only you with the horns on your forehead! Anyway, you say you want to serve us. Is that correct?"

"Yes, master!"

"Okay, there is something you can do for me. If you successfully accomplish the mission, you will become my servant."

"What is it that you want me to do? Anything, you name it!"

"I want you to travel to heaven by eating the other fruit that leads there and steal the staff for us. Once you have taken it, bring it to earth and pierce it into the ground. It will open the portal for my Hell's army to get through. I want to see death and destruction on earth so that many souls can travel down to hell. All the souls belong to me, not heaven."

"Got it, master. I'll return to earth and steal that staff for you!"

"When you return, don't tell your mate about the staff and what it can do."

"I won't say anything to him about it, and it's a pleasure to be working for you, master!"

Once Quad returned to his body on earth, he woke up next to Doug.

"You've got some explaining to do, man. Why did you eat the red fruit when I told you not to?" Doug asked.

"I'm sorry. I was just curious to see if it was true that the red fruit would lead to hell," Quad replied. "So, what happened down there? What did you see? Did you meet the devil himself?"

"No, I didn't see much, and I didn't meet the devil. All I remember is people falling down to Hell's boundary, dropping like flies. I explored just a little bit, seeing people tortured and tormented for their sins. And here I am, back in my body."

Quad lied, hiding the truth of what he had seen and his plans from Doug. He continued to tell more lies, explaining that he hated hell and wanted to visit heaven often.

"That's good to hear," Doug said. "But only visit Heaven with me, not on your own."

Quad knew he had to find another way to steal the staff. He secretly took one of the blue fruits with him while distracting Doug. Then he went home.

When he made it back home, he didn't waste any time and quickly took a bite of the blue fruit. He collapsed to the ground, and his soul ascended to Heaven. Once there, he swiftly approached the entrance of the kingdom. The gate opened for him. He walked in normally, not acting suspicious in any way. Pretending to love being there, he bought himself some time for his last moment in Heaven to get ready to steal the staff.

When nobody was around, he quickly sneaked into the chamber where the staff was kept and took it. As he quietly made his way out, he was almost at the front entrance when an angel spotted him carrying the forbidden staff.

"Stop him! He is stealing the staff!" the angel shouted.

The gate was almost closing, but Quad was nearly out. Two angels grabbed his shirt from behind. He whacked them both with the staff, sending them flying backwards. He continued running and made it out of the exit. He stopped for a bit and looked down upon Earth.

"This is for the Devils!" he exclaimed.

He suddenly jumped, charging down with the staff, ready to penetrate Earth's soil. When he hit the ground with the staff, it caused sudden earthquakes. The Earth cracked open, and Hell's portal allowed the Devil's army to come through. Many demons emerged and began attacking everyone. More kept coming. People screamed in fear.

Doug, unaware of the situation, heard the screams from outside his house. He went out to check and saw demons attacking and killing people. He assumed that his colleague was responsible for the chaos. Doug then saw an army of angels descending from Heaven to fight the demons. One angel flew near him and caught his attention.

Doug asked the angel, "What is going on here? What happened?"

"It was your mate who caused this mess," the angel replied. "He stole the staff and started a war on Earth. He must be stopped."

"Okay, how?" Doug asked.

"The only way to stop this is to retrieve the staff and bring it back to Heaven," the angel said.

"Understood. Can you give me a lift and fly me to where Quad is?" Doug asked.

"Alright, hop on my back!" the angel said.

As they flew towards Quad, they saw angels and demons fighting, along with humans. They eventually reached Quad and landed on the ground. Doug quickly approached Quad.

"Why are you doing this, Quad? I thought you liked Heaven!" Doug said.

"I lied. I worship the Devil and have always wanted to serve them in Hell!" Quad replied.

"You're nuts, and you must be stopped. I need that staff back!" Doug said.

"Make me!" Quad retorted.

They started to fight, throwing punches and kicks. They wrestled to the ground. Quad was on top of Doug, choking him, until Doug stabbed his thumbs into Quad's eyes.

"Ah, my eyes! I'm blind!" Quad screamed.

Doug quickly got up and took the staff. He called out to the angel and asked to be taken to Heaven immediately.

"But first, how do we close the Hell's portal?" Doug asked.

"It's already too late," the angel said. "We must go now."

The angel grabbed Doug and flew away. Moments later, they arrived safely in Heaven and met God. Doug, in a panic, asked God some questions.

"How do we stop the Hell's portal on Earth? Is there another way?" Doug asked.

"Yes, there is," God said. "Hand me the staff, and I will stop what's happening on Earth."

Doug gave the staff to God with trust. God then threw the staff down to Earth with immense force, killing everyone on the planet in a single blow.

"There, that should end everything," God said.

"But everyone's dead!" Doug exclaimed.

"Don't worry. That should stop everything for now. I'm God, and I can do many things that seem impossible," God said.

"Like what?" Doug asked.

"Reversing time, for example," God replied.

"Really?" Doug said.

"I'll show you with a snap of my fingers," God said.

With one flick, time was reversed to the moment when Quad ate the red fruit and went to Hell. Everything was back to normal. Doug then asked God why Quad was so anxious to travel to Hell.

"He has been worshiping the Devil since he was a young kid, just as you worshiped God," God explained.

"I didn't know that when we were fighting. No wonder he was so eager to eat the red fruit. He looked suspicious in

Heaven, but I didn't realize he would cause such a problem. Thanks for telling me, God," Doug said.

"There's something else I want to show you," God said. "Take a look at this vision portal of your colleague in Hell and see what the Devils say to him."

In the vision, the Devils were speaking to Quad.

"So, you want to serve us Devils, is that correct?" one Devil asked.

"That is correct, master!" Quad replied.

"Okay, then you will be my slave and do hardcore manual labor for eternity here," the Devil said.

"But master, I've worshipped you my whole life and did what you commanded!" Quad pleaded.

"He calls us 'master,'" another Devil scoffed. "We Devils saw what you did in the future. Do you know God can reverse time? You look pathetic!"

"I don't understand what I committed in the future," Quad said.

"Let us show you," the Devils said.

They showed him his actions, and Quad didn't accept it. He argued that he did what the Devils commanded.

"You did this for yourself, expecting paradise from us. In return, you will be our slave, not our servant. You'll suffer like the others who enter Hell," the Devils said.

Quad, now traumatized, realized his mistake.

"Do you see now, Doug? Your coworker ate the fruit and can never return to Earth. He was naive to trust the Devils, who are masters of deception. Many souls enter Hell daily, and the Devils do not care about those who worship them. They use or reject them at will. Never make a deal with them," God warned.

"I understand now. Has the staff been used in any other horrible way before?" Doug asked.

"Yes, thousands of years ago. Almost no one survived, except humans. Elves, dwarfs, hobbits, Neanderthals, and orcs once roamed the Earth alongside humans but were wiped out by my staff. You're not the first to take it, but I didn't reverse time for them because they were always fighting over greed and land. Humans are the only survivors, and I've kept it that way ever since," God explained.

"Thanks for the history lesson, God," Doug said.

"I have always loved you, son. Do you wish to stay in Heaven or return to Earth?" God asked.

"I think I will return to Earth and visit Heaven from time to time," Doug replied.

"Your choice, son. Just so you know, the plant you invented in your backyard never actually worked. It was I who planted the seed during the thunderstorms," God revealed.

"Really? I thought I succeeded in creating a new plant of life. What was the purpose of planting the seed in my backyard?" Doug asked.

"I wanted to show you what Heaven is like for a good-hearted person and what Hell is like for an evil-hearted person. I wanted you to fully believe in me and be like a king in Heaven," God explained.

"Thank you, God, for everything. I will cherish these moments for the rest of my life until I die, but I promise to return," Doug said.

After their conversation, Doug returned to his body on Earth. He woke up and remembered everything. He went to the toilet and noticed the tree in his backyard was gone. He rushed out to check and saw that the tree had disappeared, as if it was never there.

"It's gone. That's weird. Was I dreaming?" he wondered. "Weird, though, I am still skinny and not fat. I can't tell if all this was just a dream!"

The following day, he returned to work as usual. He noticed Quad was not there and asked around, but no one knew who Quad was. He wondered if it was a dream or if God had the power to erase people and their memories from existence.

Chuong Van Nguyen

79

The End

Chuong Van Nguyen